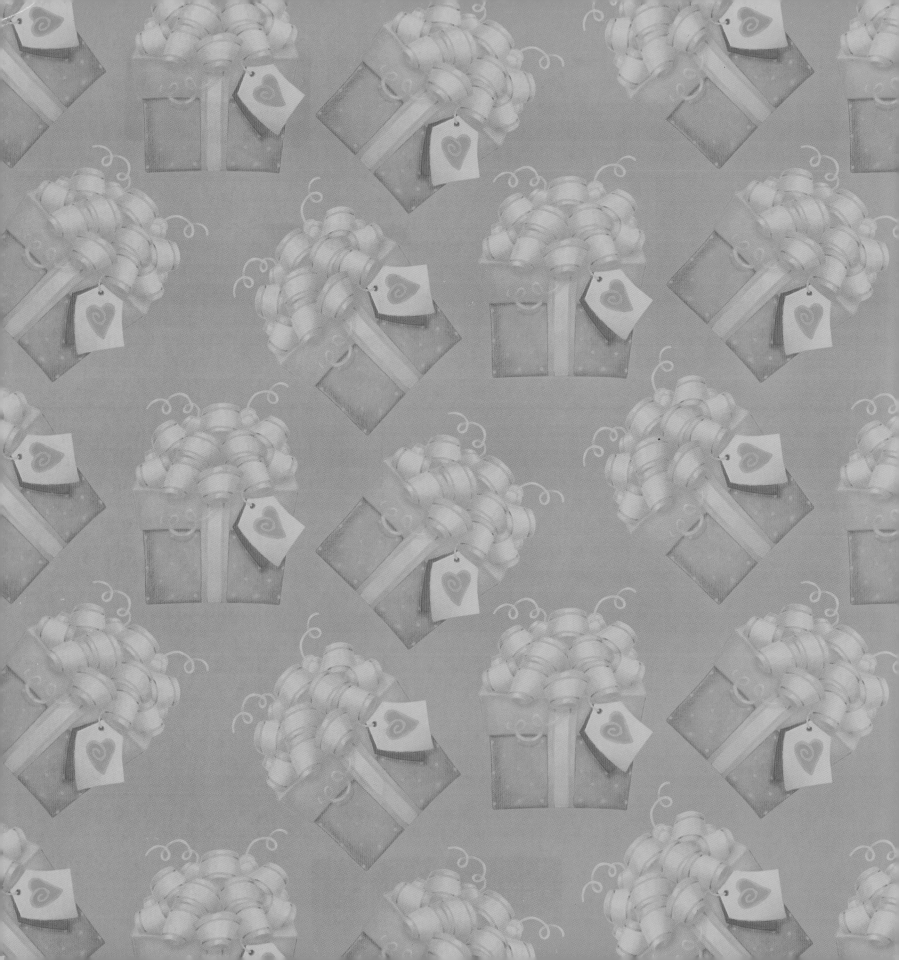

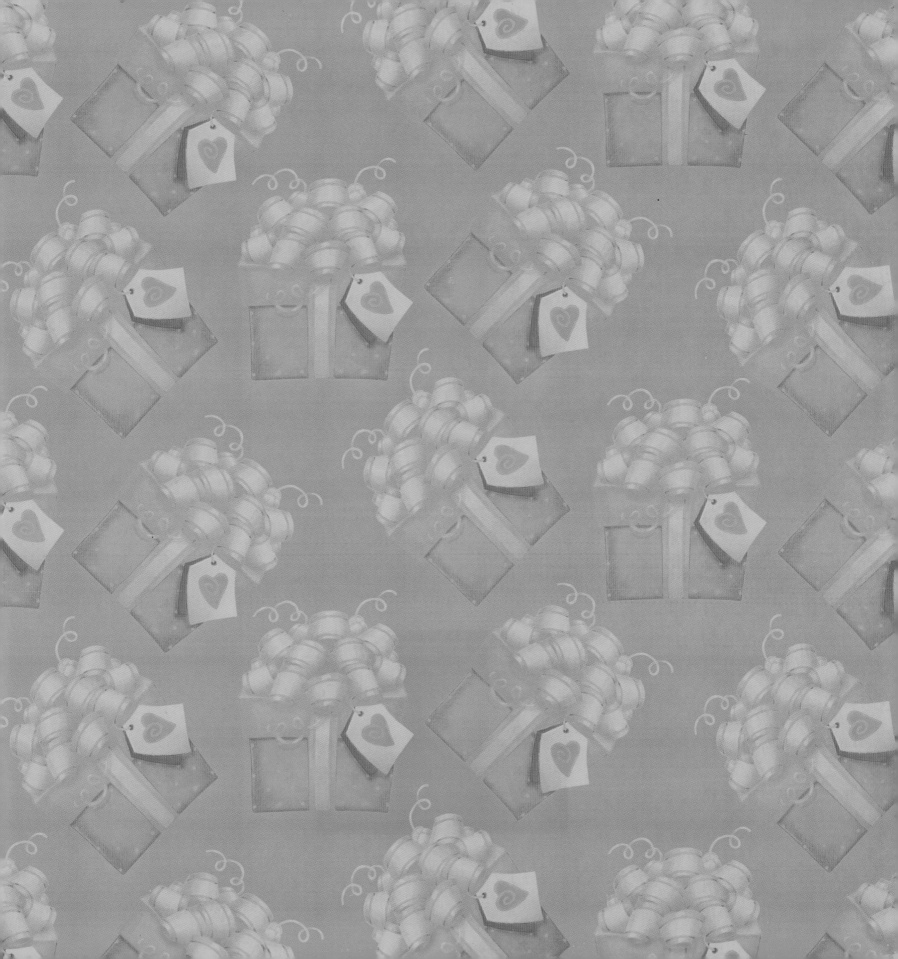

Published by Top That! Publishing plc
Tide Mill Way, Woodbridge, Suffolk, IP12 1AP, UK
www.topthatpublishing.com
Text copyright © Vincent Spada 2010
All rights reserved
0 2 4 6 8 9 7 5 3 1
Printed and bound in China

Creative Director – Simon Couchman
Editorial Director – Daniel Graham

Written by Vincent Spada
Illustrated by Steve Whitlow

ISBN 978-1-84956-101-3

A catalogue record for this book is available from the British Library
Printed and bound in China

Said The Kitty To The Cat...

On a couch was a cat,
with the cat was a kitty.
So cute, with a bow,
sitting there, looking pretty.

On the couch was a box
full of sweets, itty-bitty.
Still sealed. Oh no!
What a shame, what a pity!

'Let's open them up,
for they look so pretty,'
said the kitty to the cat,
said the cat to the kitty.

'But the box is sealed!
What a shame, what a pity!'
said the kitty to the cat,
said the cat to the kitty.

'Let's ask the bird,'
said the cat to the kitty.
'She can open the box!
She has a beak so pretty!'

But the bird was asleep!
What a shame, what a pity!
'We can ask the dog,'
said the cat to the kitty.

But the dog was outside!
'What a shame, what a pity!'
said the kitty to the cat,
said the cat to the kitty.

'Let's ask the fish,'
said the cat to the kitty.
'She's ever so clever,
and really quite witty!'

But the fish was too busy!
'What a shame, what a pity!'
said the kitty to the cat,
said the cat to the kitty.

'I guess we can't have them,
those sweets, itty-bitty,'
said the kitty to the cat,
said the cat to the kitty.

But then they heard a noise
outside, and a ditty.
Their owner had come home,
from her shopping in the city!

They ran to the door
sitting there, so pretty.
The kitty groomed the cat,
and the cat groomed the kitty.

When their owner came inside,
from her shopping in the city,
they asked her for the sweets,
sitting there, looking pretty.

'Of course,' said their owner,
to her cat and her kitty.
'Those sweets are for you!
I bought them in the city.'

Then she opened the box,
that was wrapped so pretty,
and they ate all the sweets,
both the cat and the kitty.

Then they thanked their owner,
giving kisses, itty-bitty,
for the sweets that she'd bought
on her visit to the city.

And soon, it was bedtime.
What a shame, what a pity!
But the day had been fun
for the cat and the kitty.

'Goodnight, and sleep tight.
I love you, little pretty,'
said the kitty to the cat ...

... said the cat to the kitty.